To Mum and Dad,
who have always been brave foreigners

First published 2023 by Walker Books Ltd,
87 Vauxhall Walk, London SE11 5HJ

10 9 8 7 6 5 4 3 2 1

The right of Vyara Boyadjieva to be identified as the author/illustrator of this work has been
asserted in accordance with the Copyright, Designs and Patents Act 1988

This book has been typeset in Josefin Sans

Printed in China

British Library Cataloguing in Publication Data: a catalogue record
for this book is available from the British Library

ISBN 978-1-4063-9875-5

www.walker.co.uk

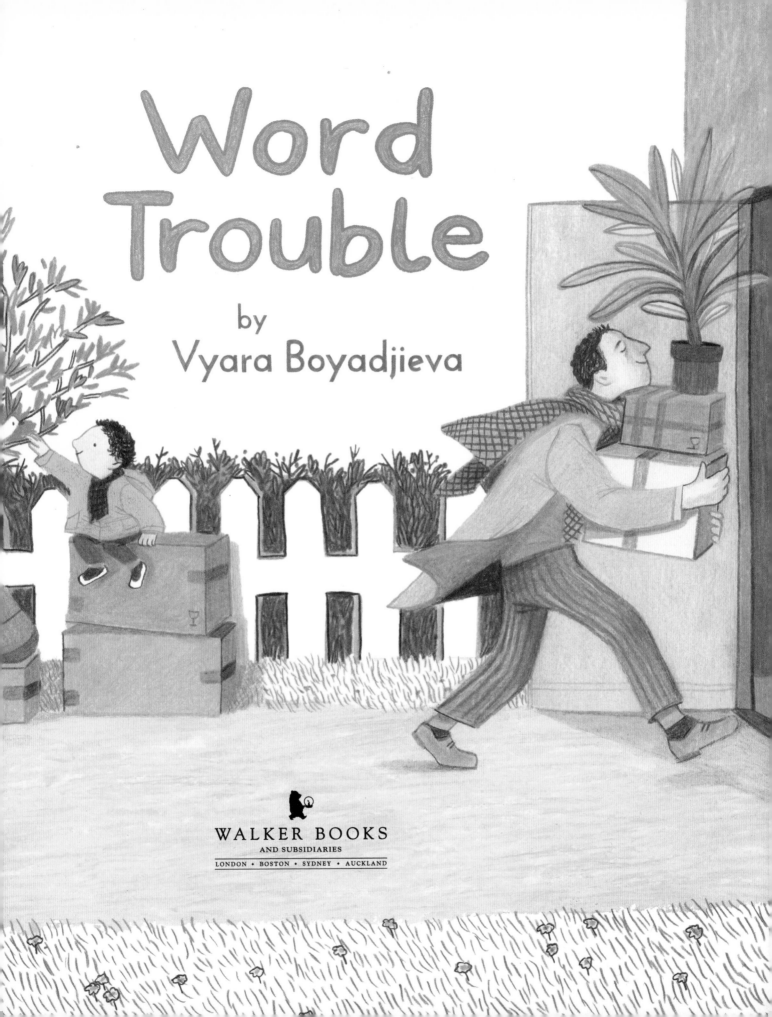

Word
Trouble

by
Vyara Boyadjieva

WALKER BOOKS
AND SUBSIDIARIES
LONDON • BOSTON • SYDNEY • AUCKLAND

Do you know what a
little boy looks like when
he is moving house?

Just like this!

This is Ronnie.
Not only has he just moved house,
but he's moved to a whole
new country.

On Ronnie's first day at his new nursery, he practised saying 'hello' with Dad ...

and with a puppy ...

and at the bakery.

But Ronnie was still a bit nervous.

And so was Dad.

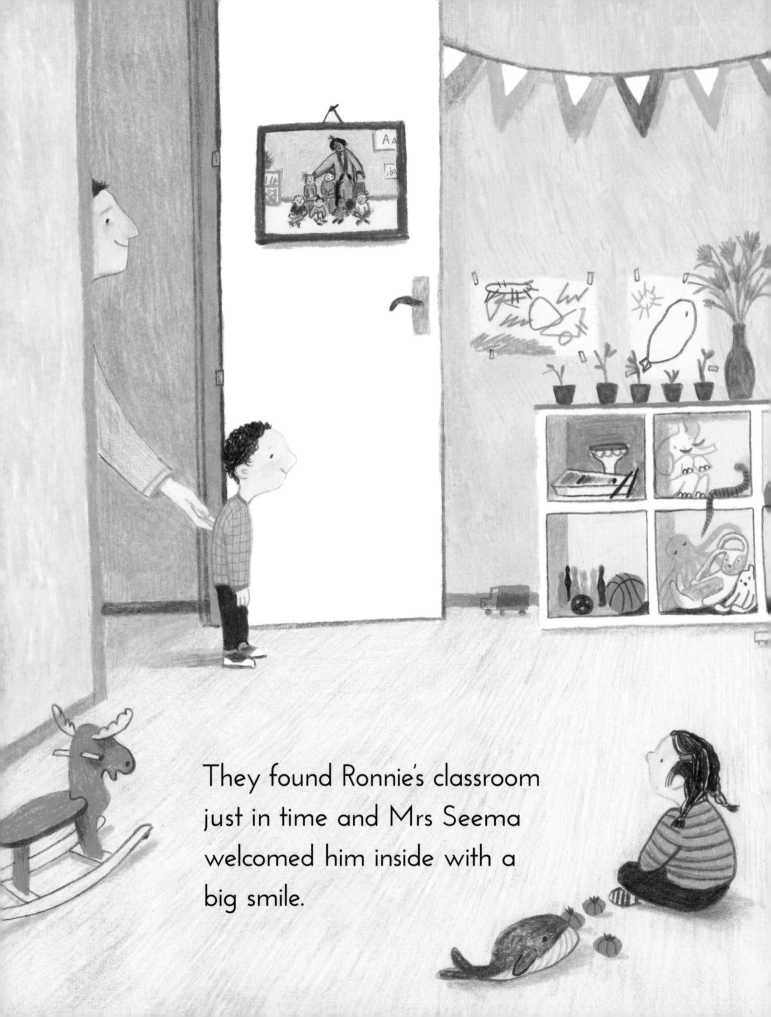

They found Ronnie's classroom just in time and Mrs Seema welcomed him inside with a big smile.

Ronnie didn't like the way everyone had laughed at him.

I wasn't trying to be funny, he thought. And I miss laughing with my friends.

Back home, Mum was ready to listen.

Holding him close, she told Ronnie that new things were scary but they didn't stay new for very long,

that tomorrow would be a better day.

And it started off great!

When Ronnie arrived,
everyone remembered him
and waved hello.

In fact, they all wanted to get
to know him better...

When Dad
picked Ronnie up
that afternoon,
Ronnie didn't feel
like talking.

But he didn't
need to.
Because Dad
had an idea...

The park!

As they jumped off the swings,
something loud, something happy,
something exciting wanted to break out.
Ronnie opened his mouth ...
and out poured all the words
he had collected
so far.

Bakery

Colo

And the girl must have understood him, because she had some words of her own!

My name is Milou. Let's play...

And Ronnie understood
exactly what
she meant!

Ronnie and Milou laughed,
and laughed, and
laughed!

hee

hee

hee

hee

hee

hee

hee

hee

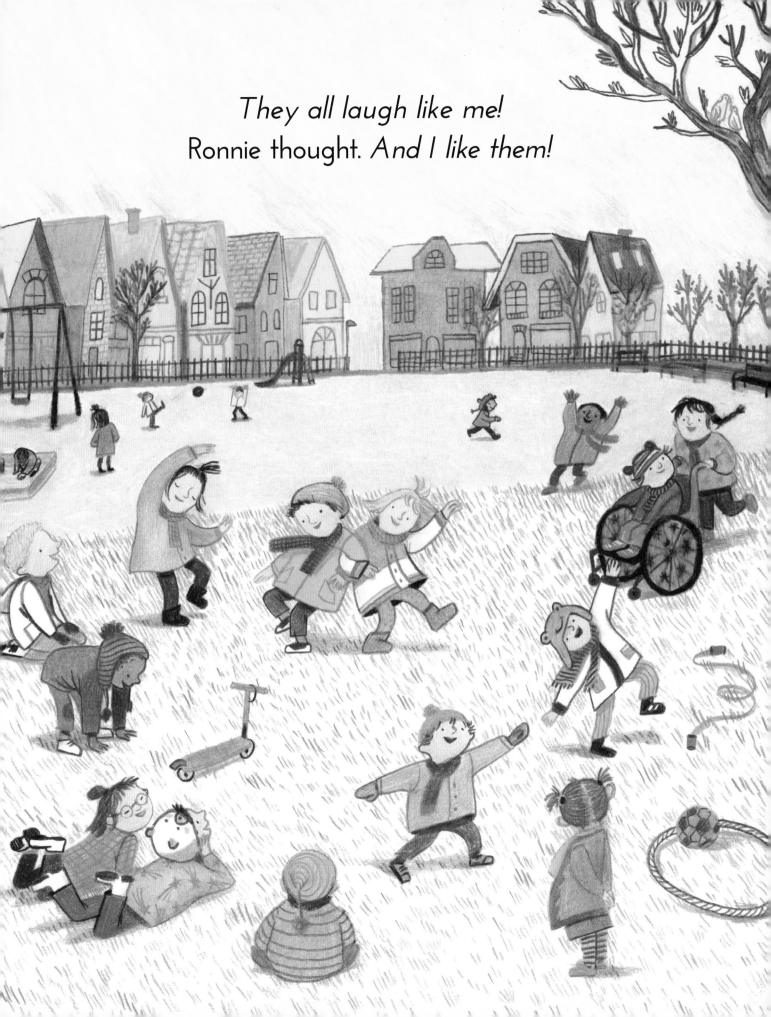

They all laugh like me!
Ronnie thought. And I like them!

When it came time to head home, everyone had some words for Ronnie.

Do you know what a boy looks like when he's made a friend?

Just like this!

And nursery didn't stay new,
or scary, for very long at all.